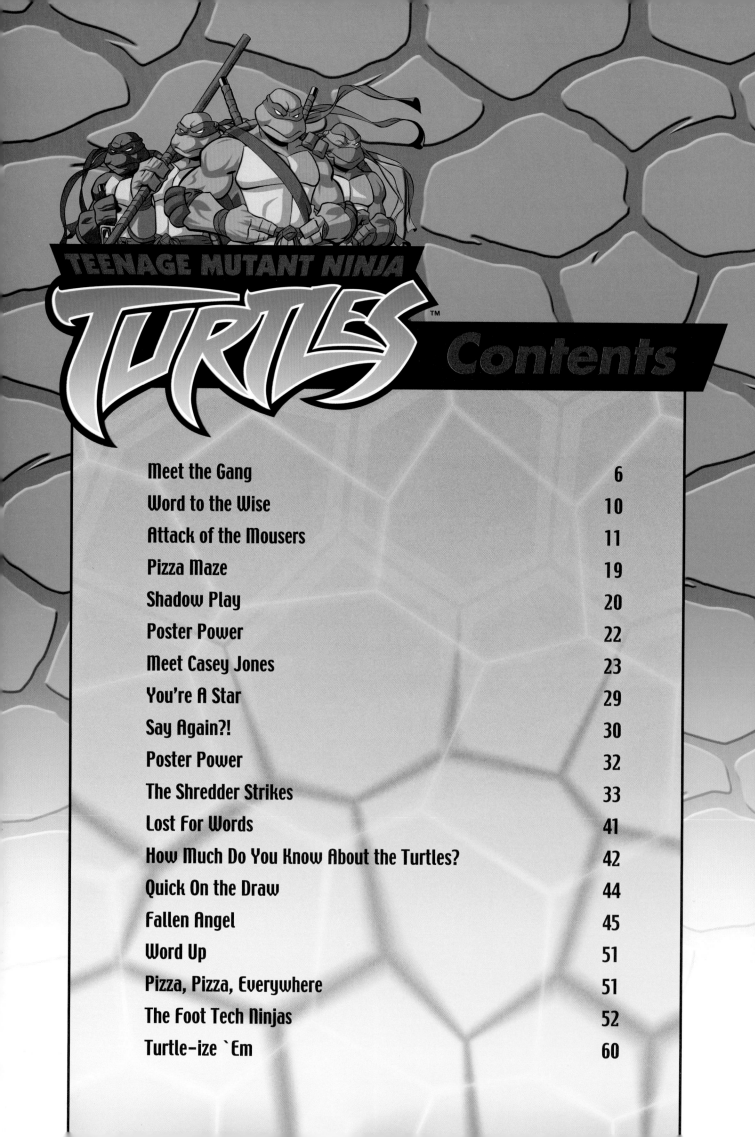

TEENAGE MUTANT NINJA TURTLES

Contents

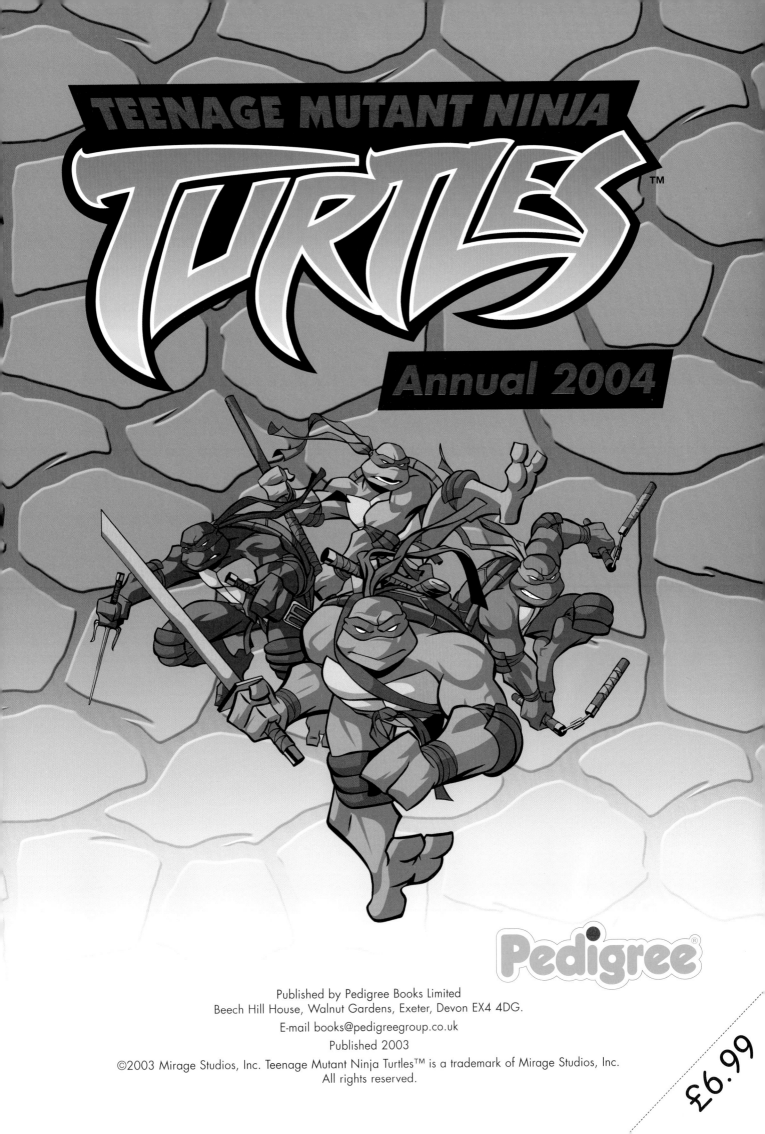

TEENAGE MUTANT NINJA TURTLES™

Annual 2004

Published by Pedigree Books Limited
Beech Hill House, Walnut Gardens, Exeter, Devon EX4 4DG.
E-mail books@pedigreegroup.co.uk
Published 2003

£6.99

MEET THE

When four pet turtles are accidentally bathed in a strange, alien ooze, they begin to grow, to transform, to mutate! Raised in the sewers of New York City by their wise Sensei, Master Splinter, they are schooled in the ancient art of Ninjitsu, ready to save the world from danger!

MASTER SPLINTER™

Once an ordinary pet rat of the great ninja, Master Yoshi, Master Splinter now teaches the Turtles the way of Ninjitsu!

LEONARDO™

Leader of the gang. Has a serious nature and work ethic, and is always falling out with the hotheaded Raphael. Very loyal to Master Splinter, he encourages his brothers to practice the art of Ninjitsu.

MICHELANGELO™

The party dude, the class clown, and the most athletic of the team. Always ready with a joke and a one-liner. Tries to keep the peace between Leonardo and Raphael.

GANG!

DONATELLO™

The team's genius inventor, builds and creates high-tech devices such as the Battle Shell and the Sewer Sled. Quiet and withdrawn, he prefers to spend time alone rather than interacting with the group.

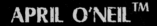

RAPHAEL™

An impetuous, hot-tempered rebel, who prefers to fight than sort out problems peacefully. The toughest of the team, but his bad moods do tend to get everyone into trouble!

APRIL O'NEIL™

April used to work as the lab assistant for the mad scientist Dr. Baxter Stockman, and now runs her own antique store. She's the Turtles' 'Big Sister', and is always there when the team needs her.

CASEY JONES

A completely mad vigilante, Casey's temper is even worse than Raphael's! He wants revenge on Hun and the Purple Dragons gang for what they did to his father in the past. Not a man to have as an enemy!

MEET THE GANG!

SHREDDER™

Oroku Saki - Shredder! - is evil beyond words! Saki pretends to be a successful businessman, but as the Shredder he is the most feared criminal in the world! Oh, yeah, and he HATES the Turtles!

THE FOOT

Well-organised crime ring, led by the Shredder. There are many different divisions from corporate criminals to the deadly Foot Ninja warriors!

HUN

The Shredder's right hand man. A mountain of pure power, he knows almost as much about Ninjitsu as Shredder himself! Looks on Shredder as his own father!

THE PURPLE DRAGONS GANG

Toughest, if most stupid street gang in New York City. The Foot's lowest level manpower, handling such tasks as shakedowns, protection rackets and petty crime.

BAXTER STOCKMAN

Stockman runs the successful StockTronics Inc. technology company. A mad yet genius evil scientist, who occasionally works for Shredder!

WORD
TO THE WISE!

Hi, Turtle fans! Donatello here! When I'm not busy inventing new vehicles and machines for my brothers and I to use in our fight against the Shredder, I take some downtime by completing my favourite puzzles!

Can you put the names below into the word grid? The highlighted letters will spell a hidden name! I've included one of the names to start you off!

3 Letters
Hun

4 Letters
Foot

5 Letters
April
Casey

6 Letters
Baxter

7 Letters
Mousers
Raphael
Turtles

8 Letters
Leonardo
Shredder
Splinter

CASEY

10

ATTACK OF THE MOUSERS!

Cowabunga, dudes! Donatello here. Wanna know where the Teenage Mutant Ninja Turtles came from, and how we became such good friends with April O'Neil...? Well, read on...!

It all started in our old sewer lair under New York City, one we'd lived in for fifteen years, and where we had been brought up and trained in the art of Ninjitsu by our Sensei, Master Splinter. (He's a giant talking rat – hey, like I can talk!)

Anyway, there we were, busy practising our Ninjitsu powers of stealth and secrecy, learning to become shadow warriors, when our lair started collapsing all around us! KKKRRRAAAKKAAADOOOM!

At first we thought it was an earthquake, but no, it was – no kidding! – dozens of robot mice, eating their way through concrete and steel, and swarming into our home!

Of course, Leonardo, Michelangelo Raphael and I immediately jumped into a defensive stance, ready for action!

"What are those things?" gasped Leonardo, puzzled.

"New York cockroaches?" quipped Michelangelo.

"Whatever they are," Raphael yelled angrily, whipping out his two single-pronged sai blades before leaping to attack, "they've picked the wrong party to crash! Haaaiiii-yah!"

He quickly showed those intruders some...Turtle Power! Yet these things were so tough, his blows simply bounced off them!

And these robotic nightmares just kept on coming, chomping through walls, support columns, furniture – you name it, they were out to destroy it!

Well, we couldn't let Raphael have all the fun. I twirled my bo staff, knocking them flying, Leonardo swept them aside with his twin katana swords while Michelangelo spun his nunchaku – we were giving 'em shell!

Trouble was, even though we were smashing these creatures into so much electrical junk, they'd already done a job on our home. With a loud KKKRRRAAASSSSSHH!! the sewers collapsed all around us!

"Goodbye, home sweet home," groaned Mikey, sadly.

And so it was. Luckily, Master Splinter later accidentally discovered a high, multi-levelled, multi-tunnelled chamber deep underground which was perfect for us to turn into our new lair! Hey, you can't keep a good Turtle down!

While we were doing up the place, Mikey was watching news coverage on our Monitor Wall. It caught all our attentions!

"...In a press conference today at StockTronics Inc.," the reporter was saying. "Founder and CEO Dr. Baxter Stockman was on hand to unveil his latest innovation..."

They showed Stockman at a podium, revealing his invention for getting rid of the city's rat population. "I give you," he declared, triumphantly. "the StockTronics 'Mouser'!"

Guess what? It was the same rotten robots that had destroyed our old lair!

Raphael knew exactly what we should do. "I say we head over to StockTronics Inc. and kick some serious shell!" he growled.

It was then that we saw April O'Neil for the first time, standing next to Stockman. She was his young lab assistant, and she admired him greatly.

However, later that evening, she made a discovery that would soon change her mind about her genius boss!

Already suspicious of his motives for

inventing the Mousers, and learning that he had accidentally lost some in a trial run (those were the ones that had trashed our place!) she listened in on a conversation Stockman was having by vid screen with someone who would one day turn out to be our greatest enemy – Shredder!

"I've already upgraded the Mousers for greater durability," Stockman was saying. "I assure you they will perform flawlessly for the next phase of the plan."

"They had better, Stockman," hissed Shredder, threateningly. "For your sake!"

Meantime, I had got one of the Mousers we'd destroyed working again – unfortunately, it then got away from me! Me and my brothers were chasing it through the tunnels, the Mouser skittering ahead of us. We almost caught up with it when it began chomping through a tunnel wall! "C'mon!" I said, urgently, following it through the hole it had created.

Trouble was, the critter had eaten through the pipe's main supports. The large pipe above us came crashing down, releasing a torrent of water that swept us all off our feet!

"Woaaaaahh!" we all cried, thrashing around in a wild water ride through the tunnel. We were headed straight for the tunnel mouth, and a huge waterfall drop that would send us tumbling into the drainage junction and a deadly roiling whirlpool below!

"Grab on!" I yelled, whipping out my bo staff and thrusting it into a grate in the wall, just before we were thrown over the edge of the waterfall!

Leonardo grabbed hold of my legs as he went over the side, Raph grabbed Leo's legs and Mikey Raph's, and there we were, dangling like a turtle chain over the waterfall. If we fell, it was turtle soup for the lot of us...!

"I've got an idea!" shouted Mikey, swinging himself, Leo and Raph straight into and under the waterfall. Then there was nothing...but silence...!

P'tooy

"Guys!" I shouted in alarm. "You okay?" Behind the waterfall, my brothers were clinging to the wall by use of their shuriken jammed into the brickwork.

"P'tooy!" Raph spluttered. "Peachy!"

Back at StockTronics Inc., April had discovered a secret subterranean warehouse facility, where hundreds of Mousers were stockpiled.

"What are you really up to, Stockman?" she muttered darkly, from a balcony overlooking the warehouse floor.

"That would be telling, Miss O'Neil," said Stockman, emerging from the shadows. "Suffice to say, my army of Mousers will make me a very rich and powerful man."

He grabbed a joystick near a computer terminal. An assembly line servo arm whirred down, grabbing hold of April and dropping her into the centre of the Mousers.

"I'm afraid I can't let you live, Miss O'Neil" hissed Stockman. "You've seen far too much already!"

He entered a command into the computer terminal and the Mousers sprang to life, their ravenous jaws snapping menacingly at April. She dived through an access tunnel exit, the Mousers chasing after her.

Inside the tunnel, April ducked into one of the many smaller sewer pipes, the Mousers hot on her trail...!

Which is where we came in! Having saved ourselves, we heard April screaming in terror. The Mousers had caught up with her, threatening to tear her apart. Well, rescuing people in distress is just what we've been trained for!

Following the screams, we discovered April trapped by the Mousers. My bo staff knocked the heads off some of them, Mikey's twirling nunchaku some more! **WHACCK! WHAAM!** Raph impaled more with his sai blades, while Leo finished off the rest with his whirling katana swords! **THUDD! SLICE!**

"Oh, thank you," gasped April, when the last Mouser fell. "You saved my...my...!" Then she saw us up close – and fainted in shock, falling into Michelangelo's arms.

"So," he said, hopefully. "Can I keep her?"

Master Splinter was none too pleased about us bringing April back to our lair, but once she had recovered, she promised never to reveal the existence of giant, three-fingered turtles and a giant talking rat to anyone. As she said, who would believe her?!

"If I'm keeping your secret," she said, smiling. "What exactly is it?"

And so, for the first time ever, a human heard the secret origin of the Turtles...!

Master Splinter told her how he was once a normal rat, doing what rats normally do, sniffing around garbage. He witnessed an accident, a blind man crossing the street, almost run down by a truck.

"A young boy was also crossing the street," he went on. "He carried a glass jar with four pet infant turtles inside."

The boy was jostled by a teenager, who pushed the old man out of the way of danger and the boy dropped the jar, which smashed open on the ground.

"As the truck swerved," continued our Sensei. "a metal canister bounced out of the back."

The canister and the turtles were washed down a storm drain, where the canister also crashed open, covering the turtles with glowing ooze. The rat took pity on the baby turtles and rescued them, getting covered in the ooze himself.

"The next morning I awoke to find the four had doubled in size," said Master Splinter to an awed April. "The ooze had affected their growth. It changed me as well, making me larger and more intelligent."

Realising that the world is a dangerous place, Sensei taught us Ninjitsu, choosing names for us from a book of Renaissance art.

"So we have remained in secret," Master Splinter finished. "And that is our story."

Just then, Michelangelo caught a news report on our Monitor Wall. A bank robbery had taken place, video footage showed the chewed floor of a vault, the bank's security boxes torn open. The teeth marks on the twisted metal were sure signs of Mouser work!

"This must be what I heard Dr Stockman talking about," gasped April. "He's got the Mousers robbing banks!"

Raphael growled through gritted teeth. "I say we shut down Mouser central. Permanently!"

That night, we broke into StockTronics Inc. through the sewer system...!

Once inside, April shut down the security cameras, allowing us to use our shadow stealth abilities to reach the Mouser assembly lab undetected. Above us was a long assembly line equipped with a row of industrial lasers on robotic arms.

"This is too quiet," said a worried Leonardo, right before the lab doors slammed shut!

"Intruders...here to steal my secrets?" hissed Stockman, looking down at us from a glass-panelled control room. "You'll leave here with nothing...not even your lives!"

And with that, he set the lasers blazing...directly in our path!

But we ain't Ninja Turtles for nothing! Leaping and spinning in the air, my brothers deflected the laser beams with their weapons, allowing me to reach the control panel of one of the lasers. Cross-connecting wires, I swung it around, and the deadly beam blasted the other lasers, destroying them all! ZZZZZZKKK!!

Moments later, we had smashed our way into the control room. April quickly joined us, much to Stockman's surprise.

"I've got enough evidence to put you away for years," she told him.

"Too late!" smirked Stockman. "I've recalled the Mouser horde. They'll be here any second. They'll tear you to pieces!"

A wave of Mousers appeared out of the darkness, swarming over us!

While April and I frantically tried to shut them down, typing furiously at the computer consoles, Leo, Mikey and Raph battled bravely, punching and slicing and hitting and whacking with all their strength. But it was no use!

"This is it!" growled Raphael, as more Mousers appeared. "It's been fun, guys!"

April had just typed in a final command. She hit the ENTER key and...! All the Mousers froze! Phew!

"Good work, April," I said, proudly. "I've never seen anything like that."

But she had bad news. "The only way I could stop them was by initiating an overload sequence," she told us.

The frozen Mousers control circuits began to overheat! KKKKRRRAAAAA- -

"In other words," cried Michelangelo, as we ran for our lives. "Let's jet!"

The Mousers started to self-destruct, exploding into huge fireballs! BOOOOOOM!

We got out just as the control room blew up completely! KAAAA-BOOOOOM!

"Here's to the new team," cheered Leonardo, when we returned to our lair.
"Here's to never seeing another Mouser!" laughed April, as we toasted one another.
Stockman also managed to escape, only to run into the terrifying Hun, the Shredder's loyal right-hand man, who took him to the Shredder's penthouse Throne Room.
"You must pay the price for failure, Dr. Stockman," hissed the Shredder from the shadows.
"No! Where are you taking me?" screamed a terrified Stockman, Hun dragging him away. "You'll regret this! Noooo!"
One of the Shredder's Foot technicians showed him an infra-red image on a computer screen, captured by one of the Mousers' imaging devices.
It was a barely distinguishable image of my brothers and me.
"These are the ones...responsible!" growled the Shredder, his Shredder blade smashing through the monitor, shattering it into pieces.
And that's how we became the Shredder's ultimate archenemies!
All I can say is, watch out, Shredder...we're gonna turtle-ize ya!

PIZZA!

Can you help Michelangelo find his way through the sewer system to reach that delicious pizza? But watch out for Master Splinter! If he catches Mikey, he's gonna be in for it!

A SHADOW OF THEMSELVES!

Master Splinter greets you. I have been teaching my Turtles the Ninjitsu Art of Shadows, where they learn to merge with the shadows themselves! Can you count how many shadows of each Turtle there are? (Remember, they each hold their preferred weapon of battle!)

Answers: There are 4 shadows of Raphael, 7 of Donatello, 5 of Michelangelo and 7 of Leonardo!

POSTER POWER

YOU'RE A STAR!

Can you recognise the heroes hidden by these stars? Watch out, there's a bad guy hiding behind one of them! Do you know who he is?

1

2

3

4

5

6

SAY AGAIN?!

Uh, oh! Michelangelo has been up to his tricks again! Can you help Leonardo and Raphael connect the words properly to spell out some famous Turtle sayings? For example, COOL and BEANS spells out COOL BEANS!

SHELL?!

THE

TURTLE-IZE

'EM

GREEN

WHAT

MACHINE

SMACKDOWN

BEANS

POWER

COOL

MUTANT

MEAN

A

YO

DA

TURTLE

Answers: COOL BEANS, TURTLE POWER, WHAT THE SHELL?!
YO DA MUTANT, A MEAN GREEN SMACKDOWN MACHINE

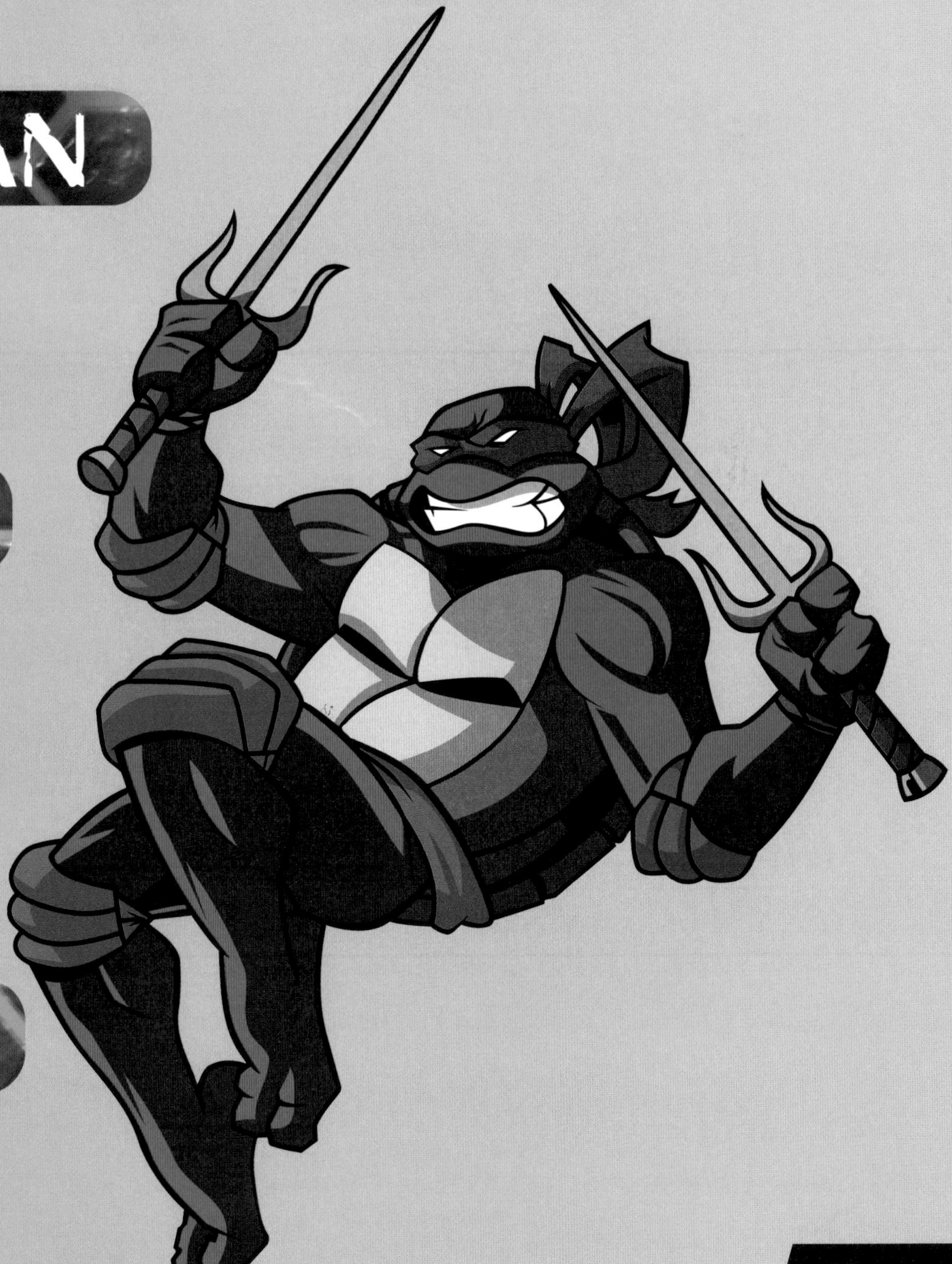

POSTER POWER!

THE SHREDDER STRIKES!

Michelangelo here, to reveal what happened the day we met the deadly Oroku Saki – the Shredder! – for the first time! Man, that guy almost made pizza topping outta us!

We were in our lair, practising our ninja training, each boasting about how our own weapons were the best, when Leonardo leapt forward, his katana blades slicing the air.

"Double katana is the only way to play!" he laughed, a'slicin' 'n' a'dicin' with his oversized toothpicks.

Before we could blink, my nunchaku, Donatello's bo staff and Raphael's sai swords were knocked outta our hands!

"Well done, Leonardo," said Master Splinter, emerging from the shadows, holding his staff. "You have won...but do you know why...?"

"I guess," said Leo, hesitantly. "Well...I have superior weapons."

Sensei frowned. "Leonardo," he ordered. "Attack me with your katana. Do it! Now!"

So Leo did, only for Master Splinter to disarm with just his staff!

"In the hands of a true Ninjitsu master, anything can be a deadly weapon," Sensei informed Leo. "Remember, a weapon is only as good as the arm that wields it. Until you have learned this lesson, you have learned nothing."

Leonardo, confused, troubled and a little ashamed, left the lair that night without telling anyone. He made his way to the

WHIIISSSH!

FWRAAANNNG!

rooftop of a tenement building to ponder what Master Splinter had said.

He was unaware that a Foot Ninja had seen him, and was even then about to fire a razor-sharp arrow straight at the back of Leo's head!

Hearing the rush of air as the arrow flew towards him, Leo spun, whipping out his blades and slicing the arrow in two before it could even touch him!

"Okay, it's not your regular mail," he mused, discovering a note attached to the feathered end. "I suppose Mikey would call it...'air mail'...!" No, bro, even my gags aren't that bad!

The note, Leo would later discover, was from Saki himself.

"Warrior, if you are reading this note, you have passed the first test," the note read. "I call upon you, as a point of honour, to meet me and hear what I have to say."

Hey, no self-respecting Ninja Turtle can pass up a mystery, so, leaping from roof to roof, Leo headed for the address on the note.

And Donatello, Raphael and me followed close behind, so stealthily that Leo wasn't even aware of our presence. We'd discovered him gone from our lair, and had set out to find him!

Arriving at a warehouse in a dingy part of the city, Leonardo entered, only to find himself surrounded by thirteen sword-wielding Foot Ninjas belong to the Shredder's deadly army!

"That seems pretty unfair," I joked, watching what was happening through the skylight on the warehouse roof, my brothers beside me. "I mean, there's only thirteen of them!"

Raphael nodded grimly. "If Leo needs us, we're here," he said. "But let's see what this is all about."

CLAIING! TWANNNG!

Leo withdrew his katana and went into high-kickin' Turtle action! He rolled, ducked, blocked, slashed, jumped and punched, and at the end of it all, thirteen Foot Ninjas were laid out on the warehouse floor!

Oroku Saki appeared, politely clapping Leo's Ninja prowess.

"Impressive," he said. "Very impressive. My agents said you were good, but their description doesn't do you justice.

"I am Oroku Saki," he continued. "Eighth generation master of Ninjitsu. Your...appearance...is very striking..."

"It's not a costume," said a wary Leo. "Although I know that's hard to believe."

Saki was not phased, at all. He had seen enough of this world to expect the extraordinary. He got straight down to business.

He wanted us Turtles to stop fighting his Foot Ninjas. It was all a misunderstanding, we should be fighting side by side against the true enemy, yada, yada...! Yeah, like anyone would fall for that!

Unfortunately, he was so charming, Leo did!

"The enemy is an organisation devoted to making money and obtaining power through crime, political manipulation and corruption on a global scale," Saki told him.

"It has been my destiny to fight for the side of good, and I was hoping we could stand together..."

Saki then presented an awed Leonardo with an ornate katana sword that had been in his family for three hundred years. Leo was knocked out by his generosity.

"I wish you to have it...as a token of my sincerity...," said Saki.

"Gee," I muttered sarcastically, watching Leo accept the priceless gift, telling Saki he would return the

next evening with his answer. "And I thought Master Splinter said never to take swords from strangers...!"

Across the street, hiding on another rooftop, we were, unbeknownst to us, being spied on by two strangers, who we'd later find out were called Guardians. They worked for a mysterious organisation called The Council.

"One of the Turtles, Leonardo, has spoken with Saki," a Guardian reported back to The Council through a view-screen communicator. "But we don't know the outcome."

The three members of The Council, who looked identical, spoke as one. "Find out...what the turtles...will do. If they are...with Saki...we may be forced...to destroy them."

Charming!

Catching up with Leonardo as he made his way back to our lair, we kinda 'persuaded' him to tell Master Splinter about his meeting with Saki.

When he heard what Leonardo had done, Sensei was not a happy rat!

"Ahh, my sons," he sighed, sadly. "I hoped this day would never come."

He told us that he already knew who Saki was. And that he had another, more menacing name. He was...the Shredder!

Master Splinter's owner, when he was just a household rat, was a great ninja called Master Yoshi, and it was from him that our Sensei learned Ninjitsu by mimicking his moves. "But, that life ended when the Shredder, Hun, and an army of Foot Ninjas, went to attack my master," Sensei told us. "They accused him of working for their enemies."

The Shredder destroyed Master Yoshi, Sensei barely escaping with his life.

"The Shredder...is great evil," Master Splinter said, finishing his story. "Any endeavour he undertakes, he does so for his own selfish gain."

Leonardo felt really dumb! "I am such an idiot!" he groaned. "The Shredder wants an answer – – I think we should give him one...Turtle style!"

That's the old Leo we all know and love!

That same night, sneaking out of our lair while Master Splinter slept, we returned to the warehouse, only to find ourselves on the rooftop, surrounded by an army of Foot Ninjas!

"Tell your boss the answer is no!" growled Leonardo, throwing down Saki's precious katana. "And he can have his sword back!"

That didn't go down too well! Drawing their weapons, the Foot Ninjas charged towards us! Let the battle commence!

And what a battle it was! However, exhausted though we all felt at the end of it, four Turtles stood tall, Foot Ninjas unconscious all around us!

"That was not easy!" gasped Donatello, his body aching from the dozens of blows he had received.

We were about to go home, when we found our path blocked by another wall of Foot Ninjas, this time led by the Shredder himself, in full battle armour!

"Those who are not with me are against me!" he growled, raising his wicked blade to strike us down.

The Shredder alone outclassed all four of us in the ninja department, and his Foot Ninjas were no slouches either! For every ten we defeated, another twenty took their place!

FOOSSSSSHH!

KKKRRRRKKOOOM!

Then the worst happened...! Raphael disarmed a Foot Ninja, the thug's sword striking an electric transformer on the roof, which burst into flames! In moments, the entire roof was ablaze, a raging inferno, which suddenly collapsed, sending everyone hurtling off the sides of the building!

I landed awkwardly, injuring my leg, and it was left to Donatello to merge us into the shadows to escape the Shredder, who was continuing to hunt us down. Losing contact with Raphael and Leonardo, we used Master Splinter's stealth techniques to reach another warehouse, some distance away.

There we regrouped with Raphael and Master Splinter, who had realised we had gone to fight the Shredder and had come to save our sorry butts!

Meantime, Leonardo was also being saved! Surrounded by Foot Ninjas, he gasped in shock as, one by one, they fell like skittles! Emerging from the battlefield was one of the Guardians.

"I am simply a Guardian," the newcomer told Leo. "Beyond that, I cannot tell you anymore. But know that you are caught up in a battle that is bigger than you can imagine. By rejecting the shredder and his evil, you have an ally this day."

And with that...he was gone!

Which is when we arrived in the Battle Shell. Master Splinter was none too pleased with any of us!

"You have stirred up a hornet's nest," he told us. "The Shredder will not rest until he finds us. I have long wished to avenge my Master Yoshi. Now is the time."

Night was slowly merging into day as we settled on the roof of an abandoned tenement building, lounging around an old, huge, wooden water tower. My leg, now bandaged, was beginning to heal.

Below, we had left the Battle Shell in clear view. If the shredder was still hunting us, he couldn't miss it.

And he didn't! One moment, the roof was clear, the

next, we were surrounded by the Shredder and his army of Foot Ninjas!

"Haaaii!" we cried as one, drawing our weapons. This was going to be the battle to end all battles!

"Let the butt-kickin' begin!" growled Raphael.

"Be careful and do not be overconfident," warned Master Splinter. "The Shredder is a mighty opponent!"

We were about to discover that for ourselves!

The Shredder leapt forward, kicking me backwards. I slammed hard into the water tower supports!

Donatello flipped over the Foot Ninjas with his bo staff, taking out half a dozen as he did so, then whipped around his weapon, striking the Shredder broadside, allowing Raph to floor him with a flying drop kick! WHAAACCK!

Unbelievably, the guy simply picked himself up and attacked again, striking Donatello with a powerful double dragon fist punch! POWW! Don crashed against the water tower supports beside me! CRAAASSH!

Mikey and Leonardo were next to fall!

"None of you will leave here alive!" snarled the Shredder, raising his blade to strike us all down!

"No!"

Master Splinter somersaulted through the air, his staff blocking the Shredder's blade as it descended towards us! KLAAANNNG!

"You destroyed my family once," Sensei hissed, facing off a furious Shredder. "I will not allow that to happen again!"

The Shredder attacked once more! Sensei backed under the support structure of the water tower. The Shredder's blades sliced through the support posts! SLISSH! SLISSH!

Which is exactly what Sensei wanted! The water tower began to collapse! KRREEAAK!

"This is for my Master Yoshi!" cried Master Splinter, executing a perfect spinning kick, breaking through the weakened posts!

Timmm-berrrr! The Shredder glanced up in terror, but too late...! The water tower came crashing down, a huge deluge of water spilling out, sweeping the Shredder and the Foot Ninjas off the roof! SPLOOOSSSH!

The Shredder fell and fell, striking the pavement - hard! WHAAAM!

The water tower rolled off the roof! Just as the dazed Shredder was picking himself up, the water tower crashed down directly on top of him!

On the roof, Master Splinter looked down at the wreckage in grim satisfaction.

KRREEAAK!

SMAAASSSH!

"We have avenged my Master Yoshi," he said, calmly. "Come, let's go home."

"I gotta tell you," grinned Leonardo, relaxing with the rest of us in the Battle Shell while Donatello drove us back to our lair. "Home never sounded so good...! Ha-ha!"

Yet if we had stayed around awhile longer, we would have seen the Shredder's blade suddenly burst through the wreckage of the water tower...! SMAAASSSH!

We hadn't seen the last of the Shredder, after all...! (*GROAN!*)

LOST FOR WORDS

Greetings, readers!

Naughty Michelangelo has been playing tricks on his Sensei again! He has rubbed out all the vowels in these words associated with the Teenage Mutant Ninja Turtles. Can you write in the correct vowels to complete the words?

1) T H _ R _ _ L R _ C _ R

2) A P R _ L'S _ N T _ Q _ _ S H _ P

3) S H R _ D D _ R'S P _ N T H _ _ S _

4) _ R _ K _ S _ K _

5) T H _ P _ R P L _ D R _ G _ N G _ N G

6) M _ S T _ R S P L _ N T _ R

7) T H _ B _ T T L _ S H _ L L

8) T _ _ N G _ M _ T _ N T N _ N J _ T _ R T L _ S!

HOW MUCH DO YA KNOW ABOUT THE

Are you a Turtle fan? Are you really?!! Prove it by taking this true or false quiz about our favourite shell boys! If you think the answer is false, do you know what the real answer is?

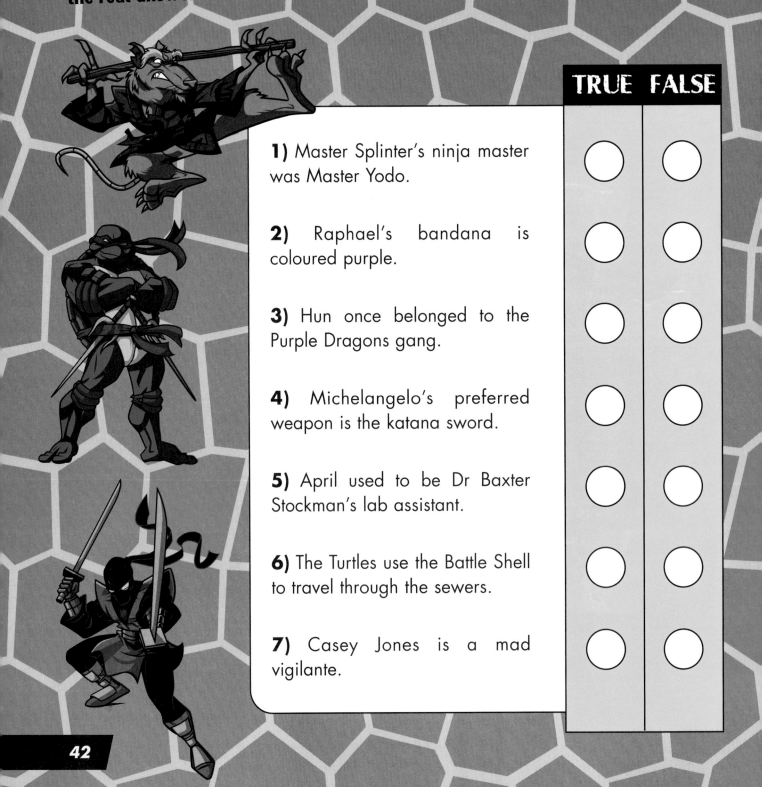

	TRUE	FALSE
1) Master Splinter's ninja master was Master Yodo.	◯	◯
2) Raphael's bandana is coloured purple.	◯	◯
3) Hun once belonged to the Purple Dragons gang.	◯	◯
4) Michelangelo's preferred weapon is the katana sword.	◯	◯
5) April used to be Dr Baxter Stockman's lab assistant.	◯	◯
6) The Turtles use the Battle Shell to travel through the sewers.	◯	◯
7) Casey Jones is a mad vigilante.	◯	◯

TURTLES?!

	TRUE	FALSE
8) The Turtles are named after famous Renaissance painters.	◯	◯
9) The Turtles mutated when they were bitten by a radioactive spider.	◯	◯
10) The Shredder's real name is Oroku Saki.	◯	◯
11) Leonardo is the joker of the team.	◯	◯
12) Raphael's favourite weapons are his sai blades.	◯	◯
13) Dr Baxter Stockman created the Foot Comp Ninjas.	◯	◯
14) The Turtles most famous saying is 'Cowabunga, dude!'	◯	◯
15) April owns an electronics store.	◯	◯

Answers: 1) False - Master Yoshi 2) False - Red 3) True 4) False - Nunchaku 5) True 6) False - The Sewer Sled 7) True 8) True 9) False - they were covered in strange green ooze 10) True 11) False - He's their leader 12) True 13) False - Foot Tech Ninjas 14) True 15) False - An antique store

43

QUICK
ON THE DRAW

Can you copy this picture of rough, tough Raphael into the empty art box? Time yourself to see how long you take! When finished, colour in your picture with coloured pencils or crayons!

WORD UP!

```
I K A S U K O R O S
S E L T R U T D L E
R A H O N A R P L W
H A Y U U A T D E E
S P L I N T E R T R
C R A O C S F A A S
Y I E N H N F G N L
C L O E A U A O O E
L B L W K H T N D D
E L P R U P S S E L
```

Can you find these names listed in this word search grid? Which name is listed twice? What do the leftover letters spell?

THE WORDS TO LOOK FOR ARE:

APRIL, BO/STAFF, DONATELLO, HUN, LEONARDO, NEW/YORK, NUNCHAKU, OROKU, SAKI PURPLE/DRAGONS, RAT, SEWER SLED, SHELL/CYCLE, SPLINTER, TURTLES

▲ Answer:
We found the word PIZZA 28 times - how many did you find?

▲ Answers:
The name HUN is listed twice
The leftover words spell RAPHAEL!

The Turtles just LOVE pizza! How many times can you find the word PIZZA in this giant pizza? The word can go horizontally, vertically, diagonally or even back-to-front!

SCORE:

10-15 What are you, a Turtle or a mouse? You can do better than that!

15-20 Cool Beans!

20-25 Raise some Shell!

26-28 COWABUNGA, DUDE!

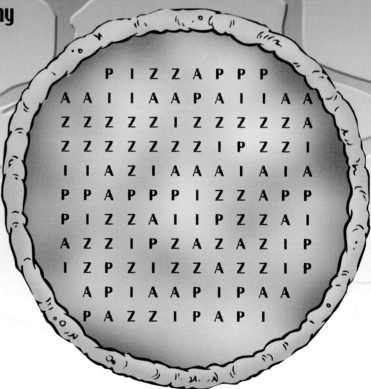

```
P I Z Z A P P P
A A I I A A P A I I A A
Z Z Z Z I Z Z Z Z A
Z Z Z Z Z Z I P Z Z I
I I A Z I A A A I A I A
P P A P P I Z Z A P P
P I Z Z A I I P Z Z A I
A Z Z I P Z A Z A Z I P
I Z P Z I Z Z A Z Z I P
A P I A A P I P A A
P A Z Z I P A P I
```

51

THE FOOT TECH NINJAS!

I'm Raphael, and have I gotta story to tell you...!

After our run-ins with Dr Baxter Stockman and the Purple Dragons gang, an irate Oroku Saki was out to get us!

"You two will work together," he ordered Hun and Stockman, sitting in the throne room of his Shinto temple atop his skyscraper. Stockman was sporting a scar and eye patch, his rewards for failing Saki the first time. "Find these creatures, learn their secrets, and, if necessary...destroy them...!"

Hey, Saki, all I gotta say to that is – BRING IT ON!!

Back at our lair, Master Splinter was putting us through some intense training, combining two essential disciplines: The Way of Balance...and the Way of Invisibility. Basically, that meant us balancing on the top of poles with the lights out!

"You must learn stillness and alertness," Sensei was saying, balancing on a pole beside us. "For they are the only defence against the unexpected."

Unexpected? Yeah, like at that very moment Casey Jones bursting outta the elevator, wearing his hockey mask and carrying his weapons golf bag!

"Yo, guys!" he called, bounding into the room. "anyone home?"

Oblivious to the bamboo poles he

WHUMMP!

crashed into them, sending us all topping with a WHUMMP! to the hard floor!

"Sensei," groaned Donatello as the lights came on. "The nutca‑ ‑...er, the guy we told you about."

Casey wandered around the lair, totally impressed. "Whoa, Raph, your crib's even more awesome than you said."

Then he dropped the reason why he'd come. Graffiti. It was all over town.

"We're New Yorkers, Casey," sighed Donatello. "We've seen graffiti before."

But not this type of graffiti we hadn't. Casey pulled out a photograph he'd taken. It showed a wall with a crude, spray-painted picture of four turtles getting their heads sliced off by a sword.

"I think," Casey said grimly. "Someone's trying to send you a message...!"

Inside Saki's throne room, Dr. Baxter Stockman was arrogantly standing beside a silent Hun.

"While your oversized lackey wastes time and effort with the pointless scribblings of street thugs," he sneered at Saki. "I have created something useful to intercept your reptilian pests. I give you...the Foot Tech Ninjas!"

A curtain opened to reveal a group of Foot Tech Ninjas, sparring heavily with one another. They

looked like regular Foot Ninjas, but with some added high-tech accessories, including exo-skeleton armour on their arms and legs, and eyepiece camera communicators attached to their faces.

They looked mean – and they were mean! They made impossibly high flying leaps, kicks and punches, sending each other scattering across the room!

"My brilliantly designed cyber-armour enhances their physical abilities," boasted Stockman. "Giving them increased strength, speed and stealth capabilities."

Sake was impressed. "Bring me those creatures, Dr. Stockman. You have already paid the price for failing me once. Do not fail me a second time!"

Stockman rubbed his scarred face, nervously...!

Master Splinter soon tired of Casey's hyper-annoying habits, and even though he normally discouraged excursions to the surface, he felt it was best for me to take Casey above ground for some fresh air – before Sensei did something he would later regret!

"Topside?" I cheered. "I'm all over it!"

So there we were, bounding across rooftops, playfully punching each other and resorting to insulting name-calling, when we heard a spray can in action. Looking over a rooftop, we saw three Purple Dragons thugs at street level, graffiti-ing a wall. They had painted a giant dragon's head chomping down on four helpless turtles.

"I don't know much about art," I growled, feeling a berserker rage growing inside me. "But I know what I hate!"

So, guess what me and Hockey Mask decided to do? Got it in one!

BAMM! SLAAMM!

Sai blades and baseball bat soon made short shrift of those dumb Dragons!

"Cake!" Casey laughed, when the minor scuffle was over, and the Dragons lay groaning on the pavement.

I looked across the street and groaned. "Don't be so sure," I said. "They called for backup. And here it comes!"

Two Foot Tech Ninjas made an impossible leap from the rooftop they were on, spinning in mid-air all the way across the street, landing right beside us!

Me and Casey immediately went into battle stance, only for the Foot Tech Ninjas to hit a control on their cyber-armour. They both faded from sight. They'd turned completely invisible!

"They must have some kinda whaddyacallit?" I gasped. "Um...cloaking device!"

Now I'm the sorta guy who'll take on a whole army with just my bare hands – Michelangelo reckons I should go on an intense anger management course! – but how do you fight an enemy you can't see?!!

Answer is, you can't! It was our turn to feel the bruises as the all-powerful Foot Tech Ninjas pummelled us a good 'un! **THOK! BA-DAM! KRIIINNNK!**

And just to finish us off, these mega-strong bad guys punched us so hard under our chins we flew straight up into the air before crashlanding unconscious on the ground next to them! **BAAAMM!**

"Target apprehended," one of the goons reported back to Saki.

The other goon jerked a finger at Casey. "What about him?"

The leader of the Purple Dragons gave an evil chuckle, the punks raising their lead pipes, chains and baseball bat to bring them crashing down on Casey's head.

"Just leave him to us," he laughed. "It's payback time!"

While the Foot Tech Ninjas carried me away like a roll of carpet, the Purple Dragons let loose on poor Casey!

However...none of the blows struck home! Recovering from the attack he'd just sustained, he

rolled out of the way, blasting the goons in the face with spray paint he'd grabbed off the street!

"Psyche!" he cried, before running off in the confusion...!

As for me, I awoke to find myself strapped to a metal table inside Dr. Baxter Stockman's laboratory.

Some seriously nasty probes, needles, scalpels and drills attached to servo arms were about to take me to pieces, slice by slice!

"Hey!" I yelled at Stockman, who I could see inside some sort of control room. "Watch where you're pokin' those things! When I get outta here...!"

Hun appeared, towering over me, his grin suggesting he was enjoying my discomfort.

"This is some nice steel," he said, admiring my sai blades. "How 'bout telling me who gave 'em to you...?"

Of course, diplomacy not being my forte, I told him where to get off. So to show me what a tough dude he really was, Hun crushed my shell phone with his bare hand! KRRUUNNNCCH!

"Let's start with just exactly what kinda freak are you, anyway?" he hissed, shining a powerful medical lamp into my face, blinding me.

I was looking at some serious pain time...!

Luckily, Casey had managed to struggle back to the lair, and quickly filled in everyone about what had taken place.

"Don't worry," said Donatello, studying the Foot Tech Ninja eyepiece communicator Casey had managed to rip off during the struggle. "I may be able to calibrate my scanner to trace a comm signal from your 'invisible ninja'. Yeah, what he said...!"

Hun was still taking great delight in interrogating me, and he was turning nasty. We'd been at it for hours, and I was exhausted.

"Who do you work for?" bellowed Hun, asking me all these really weird questions. Like, how long had I been on this planet? And what was the level of my technology?!

"Planet? Technology?" I said, frowning. "Boy, are you barkin' up the wrong shell!"

The guy lost it big-time then! Grabbing a whirring buzzsaw, he lowered it slowly towards my head.

"Your choice," he hissed, threateningly. "You can talk. Or let your DNA do the talking for you. Now, is there something you want to tell me...?"

There was, actually! I'd managed to free one arm from the straps holding me prisoner. Snatching up a still-working anaesthesia mask I slammed it over Hun's face.

"Sweet dreams, Lard Butt!" I shouted, watching Hun stagger back, a total wooz-head from the escaping vapours.

Using the buzzsaw, I quickly cut through the straps, and then I was outta there...!

A furious Stockman burst into the lab, raging at Hun. "Fool! You've let him escape...!"

Hun stood up straight, unaffected from the sleep gas. "Precisely. I let him escape, to lead us to the others. A squad of cloaked Foot Tech Ninjas are trailing the creature even as we speak...!"

So much for my great escape! *SIGH!*

Donatello's scanner soon picked up a great number of blips heading for the sewers.

"The invisible ninjas' signal," groaned Leonardo, realising I must have evaded my captors and was heading home. "Which means we've gotta find Raph

before he brings in some seriously unwanted houseguests!"

Using Donatello's pumped-up new invention – The Sewer Sled – a roller coaster ride if ever there was one! – they and Casey headed towards the direction of the signal, hoping they could stop the Foot Tech Ninjas from discovering our lair!

I was surprised to see my brothers coming to meet me, and even more surprised when they climbed out of the Sewer Sled and I saw them wearing goggles over their eyes.

These were another great creation of Don's – TurtleVision – infrared heat sensor goggles that allowed them to see the Foot Tech Ninjas even if they were invisible.

"After all," Don had told the others earlier. "An invisible body is still a warm body."

"Hey, guys," I called out to them. What're you...?"

"Ever heard the one about the invisible ninjas?" asked Don, seeing the infrared images of Saki's ninja goons all around me.

My brothers and Casey exploded into action, kicking and punching what looked to me to be empty air. But when both Don and Leo were suddenly lifted off the ground by invisible hands and hurled against the sewer walls, I soon cottoned on!

It was all right for the others, wearing their TurtleVision goggles, but I was getting creamed, unable to fight an invisible foe!

"Think we should give him a hand?" Michelangelo winked at Casey, watching me getting whacked by creeps I couldn't see.

WHIIIP! WHAAMM! BAAMM!

Mikey's nunchaku and Casey's golf club made short work of my unwanted attackers. Better yet, Casey's club kicked up muck, splattering it over some more of the Foot Tech Ninjas.

"Ahh! Much better!" I cheered, taking them out with a series of power spin kicks! Don, studying the body images, had made an interesting discovery.

"Their cloaking controls look to be somewhere around the chest plate," he shouted to us, which was all we needed.

Leonardo's katana swords sliced at our invisible foes, both exposing the cloaking controls and short-circuiting it! FZZZZTT!! Now you don't see 'em, now you do...!

It was our turn to raise shell!

Moments later, we was de champions! Or so we thought!

"Drop your weapons and surrender!" a voice snarled out. "Or your friend takes the plunge!"

A Foot Tech Ninja was holding Casey above a treacherous drop above a violent whirlpool below!

"Don't do it!" shouted Casey. "I'm not worth it!"

Ha! That ninja twerp wasn't the only one who could play the vanishing game. While we kept him busy talking, Michelangelo slipped into the shadows.

"The Way of Balance...the Way of Invisibility," he hummed, remembering Master Splinter's words.

Climbing to the top of a narrow pipe, he perched precariously above the Foot Tech Ninja...and them dropped!

POW! The creep was floored!

"Waaah!" Casey went over the edge, falling towards the roiling waters below!

THWWIIIIP! Donatello's thrust out his bo staff, snagging Casey by his shirt and reeling him in!

BIFF! BLAAMM! THWAAAMMM! Leonardo and I finished off the few remaining Foot Tech Ninjas still standing!

"Thanks, guys," said Casey, after the goons did a runner outta the sewers. "I owe you."

"We take cash, personal cheques and most major credit cards," laughed Michelangelo, holding out his hand!

TURTLE-IZE 'EM!

This is a thrilling game for two players! Flip a coin to see who is going to be on the Turtles' side, and who is going to fight for The Shredder. Choose the name of one of the characters listed beside each fight ring, and then take it in turn to write the first letter(s) of that name into one of the squares of the relevant fight ring grid. For instance, 'MS' for Master Spinter or 'S' for Saki.

Whoever links three squares in a row with their letters, across, down or diagonally, wins that battle. If neither of you succeeds, that battle is declared drawn. Once the squares of one fight ring have been filled, move onto the next one. The winner is the person who wins the most battles!

RAPHAEL vs HUN

LEONARDO v PURPLE DRAG

SPLINTER vs SAKI

MICHELANGELO vs FOOT

DONATELLO vs SHREDDER